LONE WOLF and CUB

by KAZUO KOIKE and GOSEKI KOJIMA

cover by FRANK MILLER and LYNN VARLEY

第8巻

小池一夫

小島剛夕

Kazuo Koike — STORY **Goseki Kojima** — ART

Frank Miller
COVER ILLUSTRATION & INTRODUCTION

David Lewis, Christine M. Martine, Alex Wald
ENGLISH ADAPTATION

Willie Schubert — LETTERING **Paul Guinan** — PRODUCTION

Rick Oliver — EDITOR Rick Obadiah — PUBLISHER

Alex Wald — ART DIRECTOR Kathy Kotsivas — OPERATIONS DIRECTOR

Rick Taylor — PRODUCTION MANAGER Kurt Goldzung — SALES DIRECTOR

Lone Wolf and Cub (Kozure Okami) © 1987 Kazuo Koike and Goseki Kojima.

English translation © 1987 First Comics, Inc. and Global Communications Corporation.

Cover illustration and introduction © 1987 Frank Miller.

Published monthly in the United States of America by First Comics, Inc., 435 N. LaSalle, Chicago Il 60610, and Studio Ship, Inc. under exclusive license by Global Communications Corporation, Musashiya Building, 4th Floor, 27-10, Aobadai 1-Chome, Meguro-Ku, Tokyo, 153 Japan, owner of world wide publishing rights to the property Lone Wolf and Cub.

Lone Wolf and Cub #8 (ISBN 0-915419-17-3) © 1987 First Comics, Inc. and Global Communications Corporation. All rights reserved.

First printing, December 1987.

INTRODUCTION

et me guess. The last time you picked up a comic book, you were a whole lot younger, and it didn't look anything at all like this one. It was a skinny, floppy pamphlet with a shiny, brightly-colored cover. The insides were a shade or two grayer and uglier than the comics section of your local Sunday newspaper. It was a trashy piece of entertainment, utterly disposable, of interest only to pre-adolescents and the mentally impaired. It cost about as much as a candy bar.

If that's what comic books are to you, you're not alone. Most comic books published in America fit that description, so most Americans naturally think that's all there is to comic books.

You've probably heard about the nightmare visited on the fields of art and entertainment, back in the early 1950s. Senator Joe McCarthy rode a wave of national paranoia, and pointed his commie-hunting finger at the brightest and most creative minds around, defaming them and lying through his teeth. Books were burned, and geniuses were blacklisted from the fields of film and television.

During that hateful time, a pop psychiatrist led a nationwide attack on comic books, blaming them for transforming America's children into juvenile delinquents, rapists, and murderers. Nearly every hopeless sociopath dragged into court learned to say "Comics made me do it."

The whole episode climaxed in 1954. A Senate Committee entertained the notion of censoring comic books. Despite the hysteria of the times, the committee could not find reason enough to take action against the comics publishers. Unfortunately, the publishers, with the exception of Entertaining Comics' William Gaines, were a cowardly lot. They instituted the Comics Code, the most severe form of self-imposed censorship in the history of entertainment. Gaines took one of his comics, *Mad*, and converted it to a wildly successful magazine. The remaining comics publishers swiftly gutted their comics of any stories or artwork that might possibly offend the pressure groups of the day.

This abject surrender to the forces of suppression is chief among the reasons why comic books are as senseless and tepid as Saturday morning cartoons. It has taken more than three decades and the advent of new readers, artists, and publishers to make possible recent and dramatic progress in the development of this vital, indigenously American artform.

Ironically, all the while American comics were dying a slow death by suffocation, artists in Europe and Japan were exploring its capabilities, using the comic book to tell stories of endless variety to readers of every age.

Kazuo Koike's and Goseki Kojima's *Lone Wolf and Cub* is a masterpiece of comics art from Japan. It shows how good it can get for comics in America.

Frank Miller
Los Angeles 1987

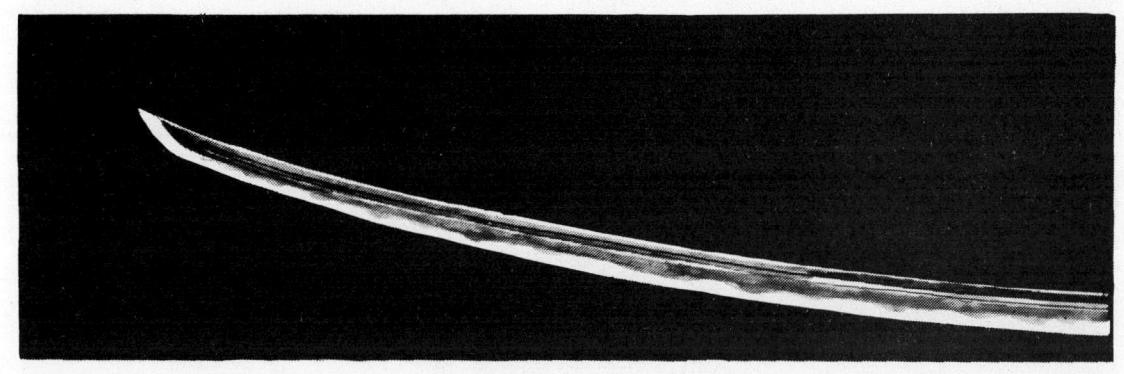

"I'D NEVER CONSIDER MAKING YOU AN ENEMY. I NEITHER WISH FOR YOUR DEATH NOR INTEND YOU ANY HARM."

"INSTEAD, I OFFER YOU 500 RYO IN GOLD FOR YOUR SERVICES AS AN ASSASSIN. I THINK YOU'LL AGREE I'M A SERIOUS CUSTOMER."

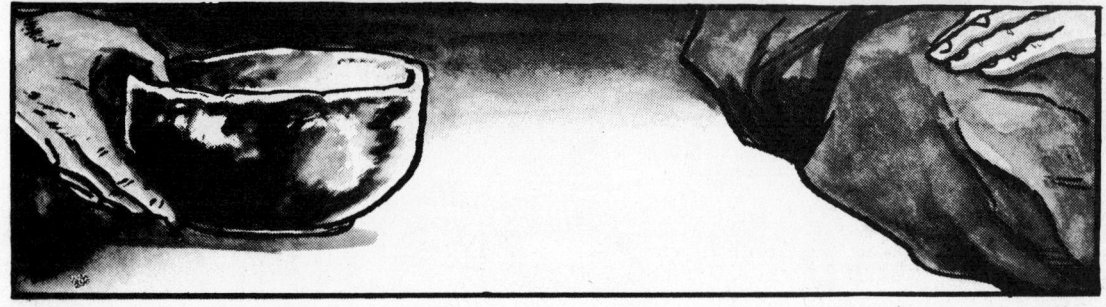

*DOTANUKI--"PIERCES THICK TORSOS."

AH!

CLICK

THERE'S MURDER IN THE AIR. DON'T YOU FEEL IT?
NO-- YOU WOULDN'T DARE...

MY LORD!

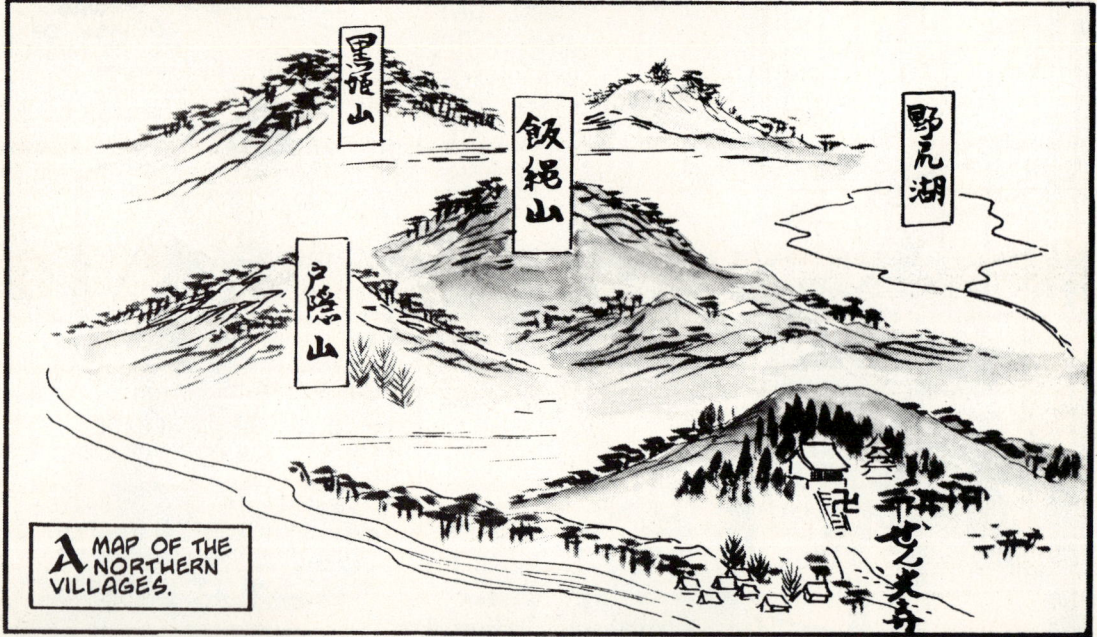

A map of the northern villages.

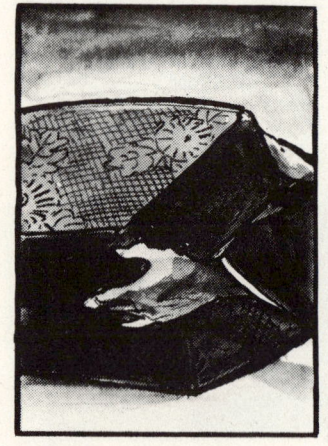

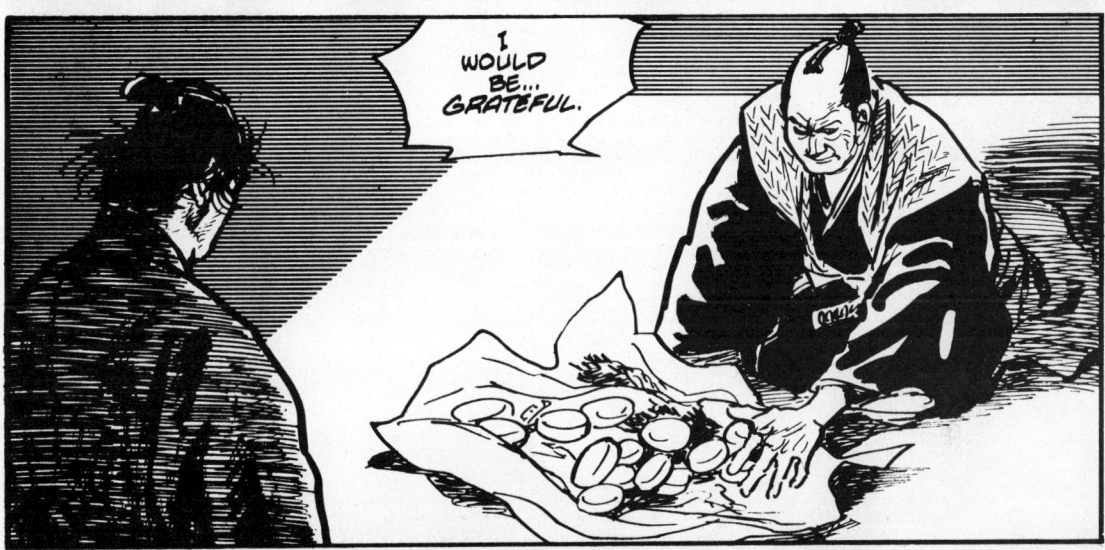

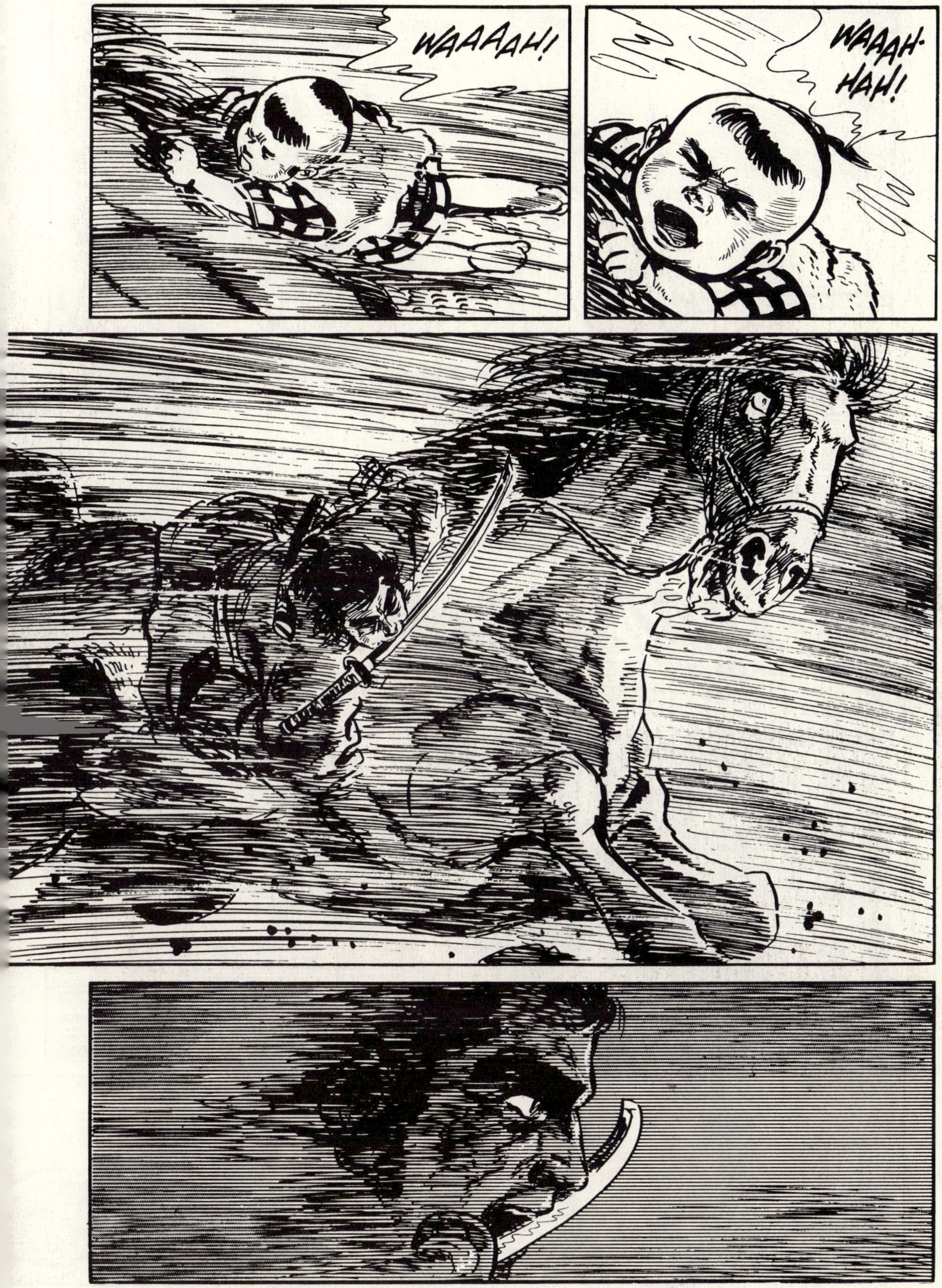

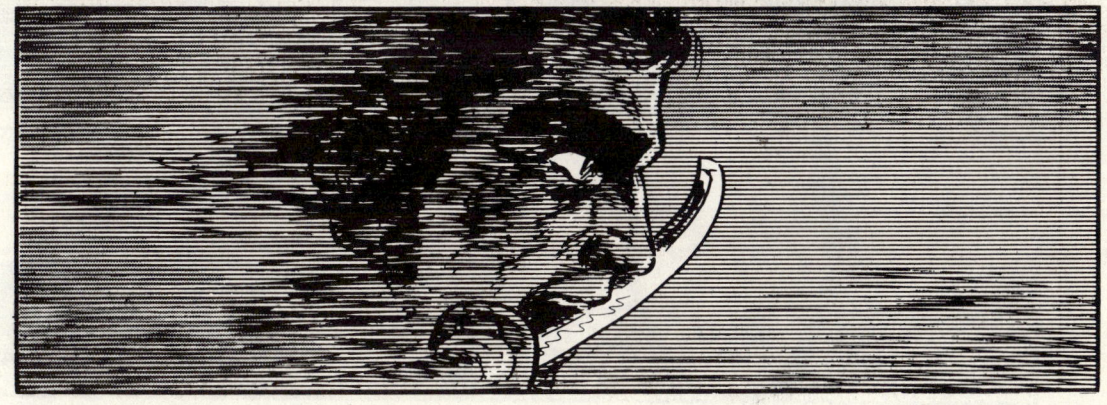

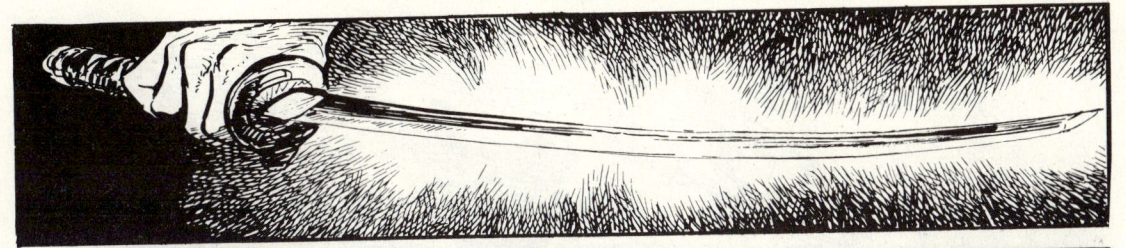

47

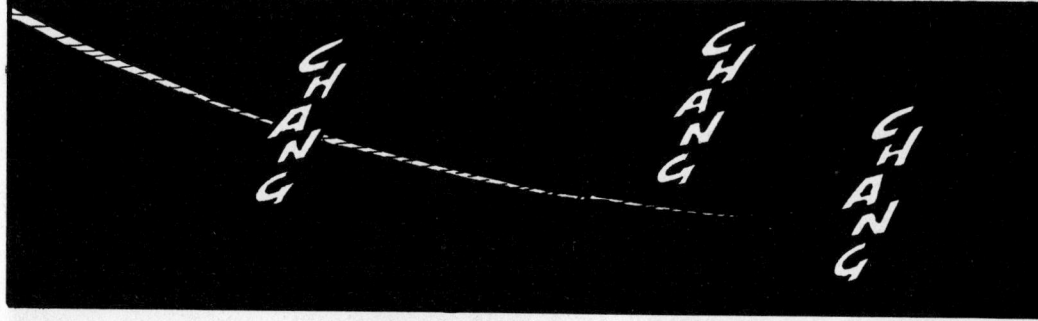

AMAZING! YOU *REMOVED* YOUR ENTIRE BODY FROM THE POINT OF DEATH!

DIVING OUT OF KILLING RANGE IN AN INSTANT! SUCH *PERFECT*...

...SKILL!

I KNOW IT'S USELESS TO PREACH TO AN ASSASSIN...

YET IF YOU HAVE ANY *PRIDE* LEFT AS A SAMURAI, YOU CAN SEE...

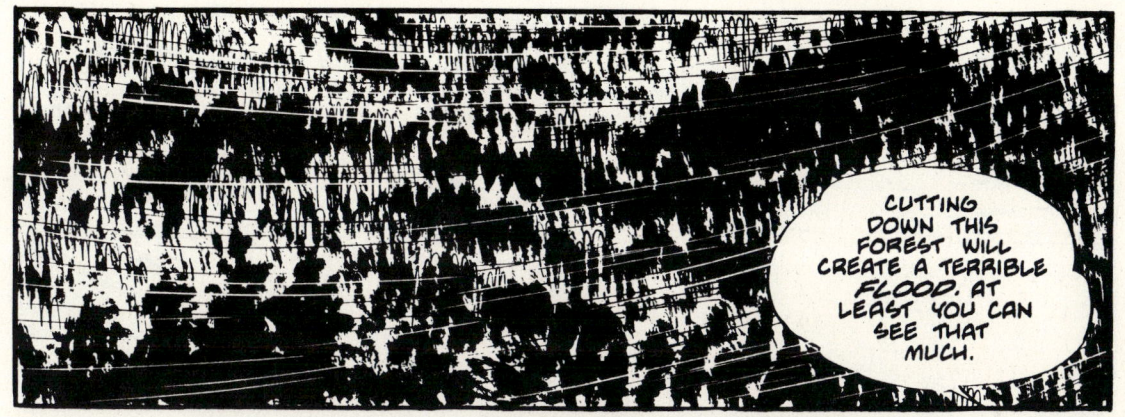

THE FIRE! STOP IT QUICK!

HURRY! HURRY! PUT IT OUT!

MY TREES! MY LUMBER! AARGH!

NEXT MONTH

In a bizarre rite of passage, the Lone Wolf is hired to fight three men marked as candidates to become the next Bell Warden of Edo. Ogami's task is to cut off their right arms — and for a Bell Warden the loss of his right arm is the loss of his life!